E
Pizer, Abigail

Harry's Night out

HARRY'S
NIGHT OUT

Abigail Pizer

Dial Books for Young Readers · New York

To my Mother

First published in the United States by
Dial Books for Young Readers
2 Park Avenue
New York, New York 10016

Published in Great Britain by Macmillan Publishers Ltd.
Copyright © 1987 by Abigail Pizer
Printed in Hong Kong
First Edition
OBE
1 3 5 7 9 10 8 6 4 2

Library of Congress Cataloging in Publication Data
Pizer, Abigail. Harry's night out.
Summary: Harry the cat makes a nocturnal foray in
search of food and encounters a number of other
creatures of the night.
1. Cats—Juvenile fiction. [1. Cats—Fiction.]
I. Title.
PZ10.3.P419Har 1987   [E]   86-24065
ISBN 0-8037-0055-5

Harry is a big gray cat with a white smudge on his
nose, a white bib, and four large white paws.

In the daytime Harry is often found asleep on
the little girl's bed.

He gets up only when he hears his dish being
put on the floor.

But after he has had his meal he goes back to sleep – until it gets dark.

When it is dark and everyone is asleep, Harry wakes up!

Silently he makes his way down the stairs, through the cat flap, and out into the night.

Not far away is an old barn that Harry likes to
visit.

Inside the barn live lots of mice.

When Harry smells them, his paws itch and his
whiskers twitch.

He prowls about looking into every shadow
and at every object.

The little mice stay very still.

Harry doesn't see the owl, perched way up high in the rafters.

But the angry owl sees Harry hunting for her mice!

With a loud screech, she swoops down.

Harry is so frightened that he doesn't stop running until he gets back to town.

Harry is beginning to feel hungry – he has not had a meal for a long time. He knows a place where there are some special garbage cans.

Meanwhile on the outskirts of town the fox, too, is on her nightly prowl.

She also is hungry, and so are her cubs.

Silently she slips into town.

No one sees her!

Rummaging through the garbage cans, Harry
finds lots of good things to eat.
    Fish heads!
    Scraps of meat!
    What a feast!
    But someone is watching him.

He can smell the fox's scent. The fur on Harry's back bristles.

He looks up and sees the fox waiting in the shadows.

With wide-open eyes they stare at one another for a long time.

The fox is too big for Harry to argue with, so with a flick of his tail he runs off.

He runs into a garden where there is often a full
bowl of creamy milk.

There is the bowl – but someone got there first!

Harry walks carefully toward the ball of prickles.

He circles round it, whiskers twitching.

He pats it with his paw.

Ouch!

Harry jumps away quickly, and the hedgehog scuttles off into the darkness.

Harry goes back to the bowl of milk.
    Even though it is half empty, he laps the milk
up with great satisfaction.

Harry is getting tired now.
    The sun is just beginning to rise and, after a
large stretch, Harry slowly makes his way home.

As soon as Harry curls up on the comfortable bed he falls into a deep sleep. He does not even stir a whisker when the alarm clock goes off, and the little girl wakes up. "You have slept a long time, Harry," she says – for she does not know that it has been Harry's night out.